W9-AGZ-670
3 1486 00179 2419

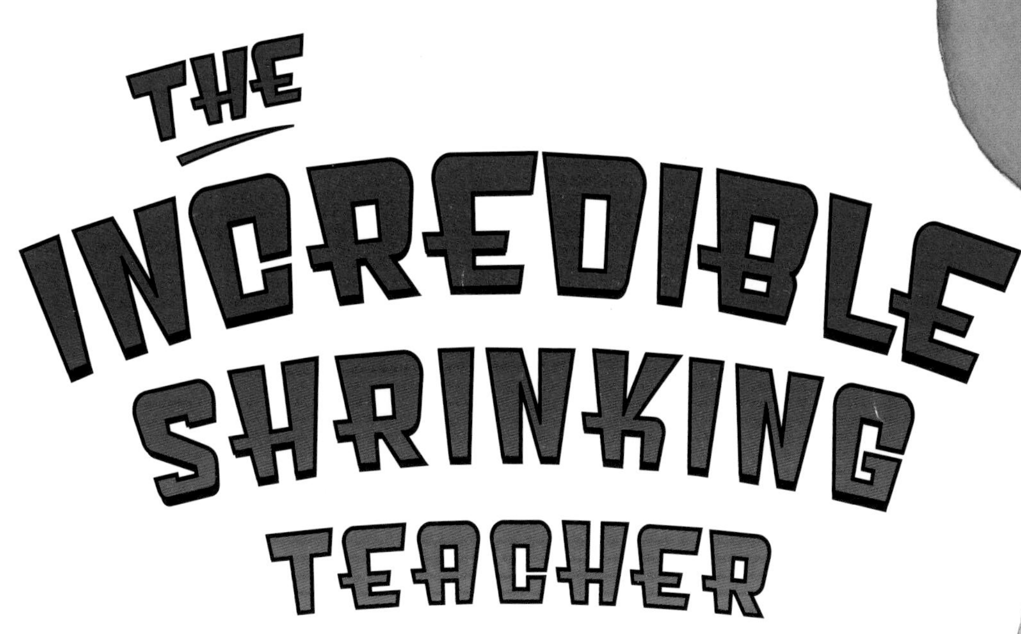

LISA PASSEN

HENRY HOLT AND COMPANY • NEW YORK

Henry Holt and Company, LLC
Publishers since 1866
115 West 18th Street, New York, New York 10011

Distributed in Canada by H. B. Fenn and Company Ltd.

Library of Congress Cataloging-in-Publication Data
Passen, Lisa. The incredible shrinking teacher / Lisa Passen.
Summary: While preparing special food for her class's last-day-of-school party,
Miss Birmbaum, the toughest teacher in town, has a strange accident
which makes her shrink. [1. Teachers—Fiction. 2. Size—Fiction.
3. Schools—Fiction. 4. Parties—Fiction. 5. Humorous stories.] I. Title.
PZ7.P26937 In 2002 [E]—dc21 2001002074

ISBN 0-8050-6452-4 / First Edition—2002 / Designed by Donna Mark
Printed in the United States of America on acid-free paper. ∞

1 3 5 7 9 10 8 6 4 2

The artist used watercolor on 300-pound hot-press Lanaquarelle paper
to create the illustrations for this book.

To

Lisa and Angela

Miss Irma Birmbaum was
the toughest teacher in town.

But none of the children cared. It was the day before the last day of school and summer fun was on their minds.

Other teachers in other classrooms were having parties. Real fun parties. Miss Irma Birmbaum went on with her lessons. Spelling. Reading. Math.

"Homework for tomorrow," she announced, "is to be prepared for a surprise."

"I bet Miss Birmbaum's surprise is a test with a hundred and one questions!" said Rubi Flint when the end-of-school bell rang.

"Miss Birmbaum is the cruelest teacher in the world!" exclaimed Johnny O'Leary.

The children never would have guessed what Miss Irma Birmbaum had in store for them. A last-day-of-school celebration! Miss Irma Birmbaum stayed late to prepare for the party.

She decorated with balloons and streamers. She placed a present at each desk. She put out a special party game—pin the verb on the noun.

Miss Irma Birmbaum went to the cafeteria kitchen to make her favorite party treats. Prune pudding. Kidney bean cookies. And brussels sprout juice.

She had to reach up high for a tray. The stool she stood on was shaky. She slipped and fell . . .

. . . right into the prune pudding, kidney bean cookies, and brussels sprout juice!

Miss Irma Birmbaum felt funny. Her stockings started to itch. Her glasses fell off, and she rubbed her eyes.

Miss Irma Birmbaum put her glasses back on. "What a mess!" she exclaimed and promptly cleaned up the kitchen.

She noticed something was different. Everything seemed . . . larger. She had to push hard to open the cafeteria door.

"Water," said Miss Irma Birmbaum. "I need a drink of water." But she was too tiny to reach the water fountain. "This is incredible! I'm shrinking!"

A light was on in the gym. Perhaps the custodian was still in the school.

The library shelves seemed as tall as skyscrapers. Miss Irma Birmbaum pulled and pulled and pulled, but the books on the bottom shelves wouldn't budge.

She was still shrinking. She wandered through the hallways. Finally she arrived at the only place where an answer could be found. The classroom.

Miss Irma Birmbaum carried blocks back to the science center and made a stairway. As she read her science notes, she heard a strange noise.

Miss Irma Birmbaum turned around. Behind her was a giant monster! Someone had left the door to the class pet's cage open. Zippy the hamster looked very hungry.

Zippy chased Miss Irma Birmbaum across the table. She ran into his cage.

And ran, and ran, and ran.

Miss Irma Birmbaum ran the entire night. The sun rose, and Zippy finally fell asleep.

A weary Miss Irma Birmbaum staggered down the blocks. "Tired . . . I am . . . so tired."

The school bell rang. Children filled the halls.

Miss Irma Birmbaum, smaller than ever, was almost crushed in the crowd.

Johnny O'Leary's lunch bag fell out of his backpack. A big, fat chocolate cupcake landed right on top of Miss Irma Birmbaum. She thought she was done for.

“Something yucky is stuck on my cupcake!” said Johnny.

“Look!” yelled Rubi. “It’s Miss Birmbaum!”

Miss Irma Birmbaum shouted. The children could only hear a teeny, tiny whisper.

The children rushed her to Principal Renfield's office.

"Miss Birmbaum!" exclaimed the principal. "Where's the rest of you?"

The minuscule teacher slipped from Principal Renfield's hand and fell into his award-winning tropical fish aquarium.

The principal thought quickly. He scooped Miss Irma Birmbaum from the fish tank. A small drop of chocolate icing was still stuck to her lip. She licked it off.

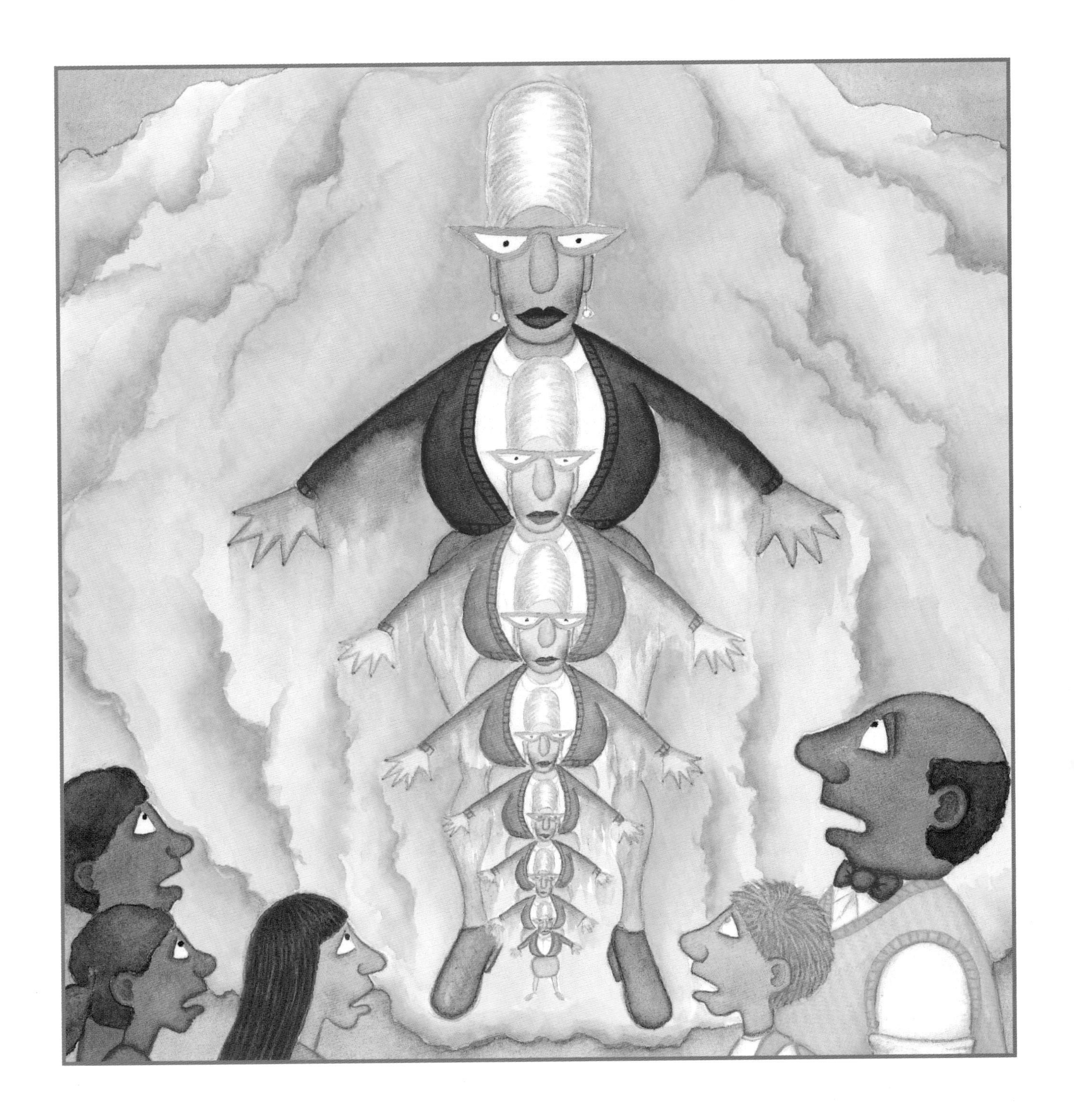

Miss Irma Birmbaum felt funny. Her stockings started to itch.

To everyone's amazement, she began to grow right in front of their very eyes.

Soon Miss Irma Birmbaum was her regular size.

"I will NEVER again make prune pudding!" she declared.

"Huh?" said Johnny.

Miss Birmbaum used Principal Renfield's telephone to order pizza and cake to be delivered to her classroom.

The children were thrilled. It was a fun-filled last day of school. Games! Snacks! Songs! Dancing! Finally the children opened their presents. Each one received a miniature dictionary.

"Miss Birmbaum," said Rubi, "this was the best last-day-of-school party ever!"

Miss Irma Birmbaum smiled. "Well, I know what it's like to be little!"